BRASH: FREDERICK

A Laurel Creek Series
Novella

USA Today Bestselling Author
Hildie McQueen

Brash: Frederick

**USA Today Bestselling Author
Hildie McQueen**

Pink Door Publishing

Editor: Dark Dreams Editing

ISBN: 978-1-939356-74-1

Copyright Hildie McQueen 2017

All rights reserved. No part of this book may be reproduced in any form or by any electronic or mechanical means—except in the case of brief quotations embodied in critical articles or reviews—without written permission. This eBook is licensed for your personal enjoyment only. This eBook may not be re-sold or given away to other people. If you would like to share this book with another person, please purchase an additional copy for each reader. If you're reading this book and did not purchase it, or it was not purchased for your use only, then please return it to your retailer and purchase your own copy. Thank you for respecting the hard work of this author.

The characters and events portrayed in this book are fictitious. Any similarity to real persons, living or dead, is purely coincidental and not intended by the author.

THE LAUREL CREEK SERIES

Brash: Frederick

Jaded: Luke

Broken: Taylor

Ruined: Tobias

CHAPTER ONE

Laurel Creek, Montana

THE RUMBLE FROM the engine of his brand new lightening blue limited edition Mustang almost made Rick Edwards smile, but the grim picture of his sister's angry tears yanked that shit right back. He blew out a breath and scanned the long stretch of winding road before him.

When he crested a hill, plush green land spanned across as far as he could see. It had rained for two days straight. This day, however, brought with it sunshine that streamed between fluffy clouds. Cows meandered while grazing in the afternoon sun.

If it weren't for the fact that an eighteen-wheeler had passed going in the opposite direction about ten miles back, he'd swear the apocalypse had happened and he was the only fucker left on the planet. Given the current state of affairs and how pissed his family was, perhaps it wouldn't be a bad situation at the moment.

This time he allowed a smile. Hell yeah, this was the perfect day. All kinds of horsepower under his ass, an open four-lane road, and not one damn call from the family yet.

Out of habit, he checked the rearview mirror. Yep, other than the few cows on the lazy hills to his right, he owned the road. Unfortunately, this was not going to help him find the asshole that'd left his sister high and dry at the church on her wedding day.

The guy had embarrassed not just Clara, but the entire family. For over an hour they all sat, dressed in penguin suits and expensive dresses, waiting for the groom who never showed up.

And boy had they waited, and waited. Bouquets of flowers tied to the ends of each row of pews began to wilt and the people gathered in the overly decorated church fidgeted as the minutes tick-tocked by.

Finally, when the murmuring grew loud and pointed looks were directed at them, his dad was forced to go to the front of the church and announce the wedding was postponed.

Everyone assumed the groom had been in an accident, dying in a ditch or some shit. Calls to hospitals and police made by frantic relatives came up empty. Some people even drove off in an to attempt to find him with no avail.

Not wanting the "what ifs" to continue, Rick admitted what had happened the night before.

And that's when the screaming began.

After inviting Bruce for a drink, he'd made certain threats.

Wide-eyed nosy guests, who no doubt wanted the goods for their social media accounts, lingered when his sister Clara topped the spectacle by going ballistic. She threw decorations and shrieked at him for what felt like an hour. Just when he thought she'd run out of steam, the little shit got a second wind and beat the crap out of him with her bouquet. Rick made a mental note never to piss off a bride. Women in white were strong as all get out.

So yeah, maybe he'd put the fear of God in the dude and demanded he man up and take care of his sister. Who would have thought a Glock at the temple and forcing the fucker to take double shots of tequila for shits and giggles would run the guy off?

Bruce. Who named their kid that?

Hell, if anything, Clara should be thanking him for ensuring she didn't marry the pansy-ass fucker.

Rick scratched at the stubble on his jaw and grunted. "Damn it," he mumbled thinking of all the crying.

His mom hadn't been too happy with him either. That part he didn't like.

"Rick, how could you? You broke your sister's heart." When a tear had trailed down her cheek, it had made him feel three inches tall.

And so now, after growing a new ass, he was on his way to try to find the weasel and bring him back to marry his lovestruck sister. This was definitely a case of love being blind. But, whatever. If she wanted to marry a guy that scared off that easily, so be it. Clara was a spoiled brat anyway.

He'd tried.

THE CELL PHONE chimed through the car's speakers interrupting Garth Brooks' "Friends in Low Places".

"Dude, what the hell happened?" his childhood friend, Tobias Hamilton, asked without preamble. "Heard you ran off the groom."

Damn, it hadn't taken long for the rumor mill to spread.

"Yeah, pansy ass skipped out on the wedding." He cursed under his breath. "Don't know why Clara wants him."

Tobias was closer to a brother than a friend, Rick and Tobias has been inseparable during their teenage years.

"Where the hell were you? I could've used some back up."

"Oh hell no. I pissed off a would be bride once, she's still trying to kick my ass," Tobias said with a dry chuckle. "I was out of town, just got back yesterday and couldn't make it. Sounds like I missed an interesting time though."

Rick slowed when spotting a town up ahead. Going from eight-five down to fifty felt almost as if he was barely moving now. "What's up?" Surely the guy didn't just call to talk about the damn wedding.

"If you have some time, got a friend near here that's looking for someone to help with preparing the herd for winter. Seems ranch hands with roping expertise are hard to find. Anyway, thought since you're in between jobs." He heard a muffled laugh.

So yeah, at the moment he wasn't exactly working. After selling his house and most of his farmland, Rick now lived in a cabin on his parent's land. He liked his life. Just him, two black Labradors, and a damn cat his ex had saddled him with.

His divorce lawyer had sucked and he'd been forced to pay his ex more than half his net worth. But anger was a hell of a motivator. He'd managed to double his worth since, so yeah big middle finger to them.

Okay, so other than a fat bank account, he was currently

without direction. Spent his days helping around his dad's house and nights hanging out with his dogs or whoever was free. On occasion he dated…

Rick scratched his jaw. Damn how long had it been since he'd gotten laid?

"Hello?" Tobias' deep voice brought him out of his musings.

"Yeah, I'll do it. What's the name?"

"Ken Brooks lives near the Belgrade's. It's that ranch over by where…" Tobias gave him directions and Rick memorized them. After rambling off a phone number Rick didn't bother to try to remember and wishing him luck finding the pansy-ass groom, his friend hung up.

The traffic light on the edge of a small speck of a town brought him to a stop.

Currently heading to Casper, Wyoming from Butte where his sister lived, he wasn't too far from Laurel, the place Tobias talked about.

Perfect opportunity to stop and check it out. Then it was onward to Casper. Another four hours on the road.

A smile curved his lips as he felt for his Glock.

CHAPTER TWO

✯

ALTHOUGH THE HORSE was content to trudge through the snow, Kennedy Brooks' mind was way ahead of them. Too bad she barely had a chance to notice the beauty of the day. It was winter, and although most of the foliage was bare, evergreens stood out among the starkness. The blue sky overhead allowed for the sun to warm her back and on more than one occasion, she'd taken deep breaths and closed her eyes. Any other time, she would've dismounted, walked to a nice spot and planted her butt for an hour or so to take it all in.

However, today there wasn't time, too much to do and think about. She went over the logistics of the upcoming week and wondered how the hell she was going to make it with only one ranch hand. Shelters needed repairs and then to be stocked with feed, water troughs to clean out and refill, fencing required mending and the list went on.

Her herd of cattle had doubled, full on winter meant more snow and frigid temperatures. To top it off two of her three ranch hands had up and quit. One guy turned in his notice to join the rodeo circuit, the other to move to Idaho after getting a job offer at a dude ranch that paid double.

"Shit," Kennedy muttered. "What the hell am I going to do?"

The horse's right ear twitched, but other than that, no answer came. She'd called every surrounding ranch asking for help or for the names of men seeking jobs. Although most were sympathetic, they had their hands full at the moment preparing their own livestock and ranches for winter.

It had taken two hours to ride her land that day to check on the herd. She'd taken her time inspecting every animal to make sure none were noticeably thin or needing anything.

So far, it seemed all were well fed and happy to hang out around the hilly land. With a hundred head at the moment, she was glad not to have more. A part of her hated the thought of selling it all. However, the contemplation of a small house with a postage stamp size yard sounded like paradise.

Kennedy always wanted a country home with land and a few animals. Cows had not been part of her dream, that bright idea was her ex-boyfriend's. He'd decided raising livestock would bring in extra income and be "fun".

Seriously, she should have known he was an asshole then. If she met a cow, she couldn't imagine eating it. Now she was stuck with a hundred damn pets. What she wanted was a peaceful place to work from and spend her days doing enjoyable things. Her current job as a blogger and magazine writer kept her busy enough. The added aggravation of checking on so many animals and keeping them well cared for was too much.

The fact her ex didn't get the memo was a damn shame. After the break-up, he sold her his half of the ranch and now she was stuck with a hundred cows, two bulls, five goats and little help.

"It's because we've grown apart that I cheated. I think we should consider other options," he'd announced after she caught him cheating. While she cleaned the orange juice she'd spit out over the kitchen, he'd calmly stood and wished her well. With a kiss to her head and a promise to "talk soon", he'd gathered his already packed duffle and strolled out.

"Son of a bitch," Kennedy said glaring toward the stable noticing a brand-new sports car. She spurred the horse to a trot. "If that ass is here again, I'm going to kick him in the nuts."

"Two shelters are repaired," Harvey, her only ranch hand at the moment, said with a goofy grin as Kennedy dismounted and guided her horse into the nearest corral. "Two down, one thousand to go."

"Where is he?"

"Went to the back to use the bathroom," Harvey replied. "Nice car, huh?"

She barely glanced toward the showroom shiny Mustang. "Yeah, must be nice."

"I don't want to hear it. You can afford one. Not sure why you keep driving that POS on four wheels." Harvey laughed at his own joke. "I keep waiting for the doors to fall off."

From where she stood, her truck was barely visible. Yeah it was old as dirt and about as reliable now as a toaster from Walmart, but she loved her faded brown and tan 1980 Ford Ranger. It had been her dad's. Although even he cracked up at her attachment to it, she was stubborn and had no problem forking over money to keep it running.

"What does he want?" Kennedy asked frowning toward where her bastard ex had gone. "Did he say anything?"

"Nah. Just asked for you. Told 'im you'd be here in a bit. Said he'd wait."

Harvey was a fountain of information. Although without him, she'd be lost. Other than her friend Lucy, who worked with her, Harvey and his wife were the only people she saw regularly.

"What's Meg making for dinner tonight?" Kennedy asked to make conversation and hoping for an invitation.

"Whatever it is, it's gonna be good. Come on over about six, she'll be happy to see ya," Harvey replied, chuckling as he walked away into the stables.

So yeah, it was Wednesday, and she always visited for dinner at least twice a week. Harvey and Meg lived close enough to be able to get there and back without feeling as if she was slacking off, especially with so much to do even in the evenings.

She kicked the dirt and considered "accidentally" kicking some at the Mustang. Begrudgingly, Kennedy neared the car and peered inside. "Brand new."

The new car smell was unmistakable. It had to have cost a pretty penny, by the tricked out interior and racing stripe down the center of it. What was taking the ass so long?

Annoyed and thinking perhaps Steve, her ex, was being sneaky and taking inventory of the goats or some shit, she trudged into the stables.

Standing there by a stall, a man stood running his hand down her horse's nose and speaking softly to it as Harvey watched on.

"Ah there you are," Harvey, said with a wide smile. "This here is Rick Edwards. Friend of Tobias Hamilton's."

When the guy turned to look at her, Kennedy had to clamp her lips together to keep from gaping or better yet to keep from saying something stupid like…

"Holy Mother of Moses." Her friend Lucy seemed to materialize beside her and Kennedy jumped. Lucy took full inventory of the stranger. "What cloud did that fall from?"

Her girlfriend looked from the hunky guy. who ambled closer toward them to Kennedy, who had yet to form a thought other than "Wow".

Piercing blue eyes under a set of straight dark eyebrows set the tone. From there he had the straight nose, full lips and lightly shadowed square jawline. She caught sight of a few silver wisps at his temples, but other than that his hair was a dark shade of brown. Wide shoulders, thick arms, and a broad chest tapered to a well-fitting pair of 501s.

With her jaw still clenched, Kennedy was sure she probably didn't present a friendly front. It was better to look annoyed than awestruck or totally and absolutely gobsmacked.

Lucy leaned into her ear. "Has God been nice and sent down one of his hunky angels? Or maybe the guy is an out of work actor doing research for a movie role."

She'd watch anything he was in.

"Shhh," Kennedy muttered as he reached them.

"Nice to meet you." Sex on a stick held his hand out. "I'm here to see Ken Brooks."

She meant to let out a comely chuckle, instead it came out

like a Dr. Evil snicker.

"I'm Kennedy Brooks. People sometimes call me Ken."

The actor-hunk-angel blinked twice and then composed his expression back to neutral. "Nice to meet you. I was told you needed help, I happen to have some spare time so if you need me, I'm all yours."

This time Kennedy sputtered and choked on her spit. Lucy pounded her back.

"Compose yourself." Her friend giggled and held her hand out. "I'm Lucy, Kennedy's best friend and advisor."

Kennedy frowned. "Advisor?"

Lucy held up both hands and shrugged. "Yep, in matters of land and heart."

Oh. My. God. Heat rushed to her face. "Lucy."

She turned to Rick Edwards who looked back and forth from her to Lucy. "I'm not sure I'm following."

So much for a first impression on her part.

CHAPTER THREE

✮

RICK WASN'T SURE what to make of the women. Even with a formfitting jacket and a scarf wrapped around her neck, a looker with curves in all the right places, instantly grabbed his attention. With long dark hair pulled up into a ponytail, it emphasized her oval face. Huge thick-lashed hazel eyes and lips that naturally lifted at the corners gave the impression she kept a naughty secret.

Her personality though was odd. Between clenched teeth, her smile didn't reach any other part of her face.

Lucy, her friend with the wild curls, was cute. Tiny and married, judging by the ring on her left hand. She grinned up at him and he could tell she was a mischievous sort.

When Kennedy shook his hand, her gaze locked to their hands and once again he wondered what her deal was. Yeah, so he was aware of his looks and that most women found him attractive. But, in Kennedy's case, she seemed more on the brink of taking off in the opposite direction than flirting.

"So Tobias talk to you?" she asked with a wary expression.

"Yeah he called me. He's a good friend of mine. Said you

needed help. Not doing much at the moment." Rick waited for her reply.

She glanced to the Mustang. "Not sure I can afford you." A smile crept up her lips, when she met his gaze. This time it brightened her face. "I mean, do you really need the job?" There was vulnerability in her hazel gaze and he wondered why a woman who was clearly overwhelmed had bought such a large property.

"Nope, but ranchers help each other out. Let's settle on you paying me what you paid the guy that left you high and dry. Or better yet, we can negotiate if you ever decide to sell."

Her wide gaze went past his right shoulder toward the stables. "Yes, well he had good reason. Joining the rodeo." A chuckle bubbled and she shook her head. "That's almost like saying someone left to join the circus."

"I think rodeos pay less than a clown job," Rick replied. "I am on my way south for some business. Can't be back for a couple days, I have to make meet a guy about something. Two days from now work for you?"

Brows drawn in thought, her nod was slow. "Yes. I appreciate any help. I'm worried about the cows. With winter coming, they need extra feed and… well, you probably know more than I do."

"I've got a few moments now. Want to show me what all you need help with?"

"I'm going to fix some tea and start editing." Lucy looked up at him. "We are co-writers for a couple of magazines." With a wave, she hurried off toward the farmhouse.

Before he could say anything, Kennedy motioned toward a

corral. "Come on, I'll introduce you around."

Who the hell was she introducing him to?

Just then five goats hurried toward them as she made her way towards a large corral. Kennedy petted them as if they were dogs and when a baby goat rushed toward her, she laughed and played with it.

Her eyes shined with mirth. "This is Arnold." She patted the baby goat's rump. "The other four are Neo, Morpheus, Trinity and Oracle." Nice, she was a Matrix fan.

"Arnold?"

She grinned. "Terminator."

"Ah."

He wasn't about to shake the goats' feet, although all four looked up at him as if expecting some sort of attention. Rick waved at them. "Hey goats."

Seeming satisfied, Kennedy walked toward the corral. One of the goats, Arnold, followed and Rick began to wonder what kind of ranch she was running. Some sort of petting zoo?

Two cows, one obviously pregnant, stood in the enclosure. With the usual cow bored expressions, both looked towards them when they approached. She motioned to the pregnant one. "That's Sandra, the other one is Julia."

Rick neared and leaned on the fencing. "Why are these animals named? This is a livestock ranch right?"

The wind blew hair across her face and her expression changed. Instantly he regretted it. Brows drawn, she let out a long breath. "I am overwhelmed by all this. I didn't want a livestock ranch. But, my ex thought it was a good idea. Now I'm stuck with a hundred head of cattle and five goats."

He looked around. "No dog?"

Her shoulders lifted and lowered. "He took our dog."

"Oh, sorry."

"Yeah. Anyway, I planned to sell everything in the spring. I am not sure what to do about Sandra and Julia. Oh and Sandra's baby."

"You mean calf."

She shrugged. "Right…calf."

"What about the goats?" He was picking on her now. "Taking them with you?" She was beautiful when smiling.

"I'm not sure. They're cute but stinky. I can't see getting rid of them though. I think a friend of mine might take them if whoever buys the place doesn't want them." She bit her bottom lip and didn't that just grab his attention.

"Maybe I will keep Arnold."

Rick rocked back on his heels and jammed both hands into the front pockets of his jacket. "So you need help setting up cows and goats for winter. Moving some feed out and ensuring the horses in the stables are cared for. Same for the goats. Any repairs needed for fencing and such?"

She filled him in on the duties, which although substantial, were not too overwhelming. Rick figured between him and the other guy, Harvey, they'd have no problem getting the place ready. After that, Harvey could handle it alone.

"Alright, got it. Like I said, I'll be back in a couple of days. Got a place I can crash? I live about two hours away near Butte. Don't want to drive that far after a long day."

"Yeah… You can stay in the studio over the garage. It has a separate entrance and a small kitchenette."

"I can help out for a month. By then you'll decide whether to sell or not. How does that sound?"

She nodded. "Thank you. It's a relief."

"Oh, I've got two dogs. They're gonna have to come with me."

Once again she nodded, this time a smile curved her lips. "Arnold loves dogs."

Great, he had the approval of a damn goat.

Now to call his mother and convince her she needed a cat.

IN THE REARVIEW mirror as he drove off, the reflection of Kennedy standing next to the corral surrounded by goats made Rick shake his head.

What in the hell had he gotten into? Maybe the work could be done in less than a month. The ranch was small and sustainable, nothing one person and a ranch hand couldn't handle.

Once everything was set up, the guy, Harvey, could handle it alone, no doubt. Or she could hire a second person part time. Soon when the snow started falling, it would be hard to get back and forth to his cabin, so he would have to be gone before mid January.

He considered his dogs and eyed the interior space. Damn things would slobber and stink up his new ride. "Shit."

A truck would be a better option. So this entire thing was turning out to be a bigger pain in the ass than he expected. Why had he gone to see about the job to begin with?

Next time he saw Tobias, he was going to punch him in the face.

The cell phone rang through the car speakers and he answered it to a husky female voice.

"Hey handsome," Tina, his sometime lover who always seemed to have perfect timing, purred in a low tone. "What are you up to? I'm thinking of rare steaks, salad and a special dessert tonight."

Now he was thinking of her version of dessert too.

And chalk up one more reason to be pissed at the pansy-ass motherfucker Bruce. "I can't. I'm out of town. Can I take a rain check? Maybe tomorrow night?"

"No can do babe. I'm going on a cruise with friends. I'll call you when I get back."

Rick cursed when she ended the call. He should have left well enough alone and not gone to see the "would be groom". Now he wasn't getting laid, had to threaten the asshole again and probably would spend the night in a seedy motel and catch crabs from the toilet.

Rick shuddered. Nah, he'd drive until finding a good place to stay. Of course the view of nothing but rolling hills and no dwellings didn't exactly promise a Ritz-Carlton in the vicinity.

TURNED OUT, THE town where he suspected Bruce hid was just outside Casper. It was homely as shit. Obviously, lovers of everything organic had built it. Judging by the signs advertising saving the earth every fifty yards, it was almost like a commune.

There were new age looking shops with bistro type tables on the sidewalk, and it seemed every doorway had water bowls for dogs set just outside them.

Bruce's aunt owned a clothing shop, with the ugliest shit he'd ever seen. A sign over the door promised "fabric dyed apparel with natural materials". It was all in shades of red dirt and puke green. What had the lady done? Had she dipped the stuff in a crapper?

The aunt greeted him. Dressed in a long caftan-looking outfit in what he would describe as a pea soup green, she claimed weasel boy Bruce wasn't about. Looking down her nose at him she claimed to not having seen him lately.

Right and he was the fucking Easter bunny.

Queue hours driving in circles on watch staring at buildings.

As the sun dipped and evening shadows stretched, he spotted Bruce's Prius parked outside what looked to be a salad eatery. Perfect place for the pansy-ass SOB.

Rick walked in and immediately spotted the guy drinking tea or something with a plate with a sandwich of green stuff in front of him.

Upon spotting him, Bruce slammed the cup down and narrowed his eyes. "I'm not going to allow you to threaten me again," the guy snapped before Rick could say anything. "I'll call Clara and explain."

"Explain what? That you were scared off? She's heart-broken you asshole."

"Would you like to try this wheat and kale smoothie?" A blonde with beads hanging from limp braids walked up with a tiny cup of sludge. "It's good for your bowels."

"I bet," Rick muttered, peering down into the cup. "No thanks."

With a loud oomph, he doubled over as a fist sunk into his

stomach. The blonde screeched and Bruce dashed past him.

"Son of a bitch," Rick coughed and cringed as he stumbled to the door. The Prius was already backing out of the lot.

ONLY GOOD THING that happened later that day was a nice hotel in Casper. Just what he needed after over ten hours on the road.

Early in the morning he'd go home, pack some clothes and the dogs. The following day, he'd head back to the Brooks' place.

He called his sister.

Clara answered on the first ring. "Well did you find him?"

Shit. So Bruce had not returned home. "He punched me in the stomach and took off before I could talk to him. His aunt said he would go home. Not sure what else I can do. If he doesn't want to be…"

"Frederick, don't you dare speak to me again until you talk to Bruce and bring him home. Do you hear me?" Her voice cracked and Rick let out a breath.

"Yeah, I hear ya."

Rick fell back onto the bed. "Damn it."

CHAPTER FOUR

★

Tired to the bone, Kennedy shuffled to the back of the house and collapsed onto a chair in the enclosed back porch. She'd not go to Harvey's house for dinner after all. At the moment, all she wanted was a hot bath and a bed.

After finishing the article that was just at deadline, Lucy had left promising to return in a couple days to go over ideas for a magazine feature and to shoot some blog pictures. "Ranch and Glam," her online channel and blog was huge, with over a hundred thousand followers and it required hours of work. In her opinion, it was worth it. Living the dream and all that, Online anyway.

Arnold, pawed at the screen door and then nudged it open with his head. He let himself in making all kinds of announcements in goat-speak. As exhausted as she was, she knew it was useless to ignore the little guy. She'd spoiled him and now it expected treats in the evening.

"Come on," Kennedy said with a sigh. "One treat and you'll go nite-nite, cause I'm done."

Content with a fresh carrot, the little goat settled onto a huge dog bed. Who would have thought she'd end up with a goat instead of a dog? Or that she'd live alone on fifty acres in the house of her stupid-ass dreams, for that matter.

When her stomach grumbled, she shuffled back into the white on white farm style kitchen. Kennedy opened a cabinet, grabbed a box of cereal, and proceeded to make dinner. Cheerios with sugar and milk was served.

Would Rick Edwards really come back? She wasn't sure he would, but hoped so. There was too much for Harvey to do alone.

She needed to address the issue of his living arrangements. He could come and go from the studio. She could lock the connecting door to the main house, but a guy his size would have no problem kicking in the flimsy excuse for a door. Why had she offered him a place?

Just because he was hunky didn't mean he wasn't a pervert or something. Stirring her cereal, she called Tobias.

"Hey," Tobias answered, sounding distracted. "What's up?"

"Your friend, Rick, stopped by today. Said he'll work, but asked for a place to crash. Tell me I didn't make a mistake by offering him the studio? He's not a pervert or a serial rapist is he?"

A loud chuckle sounded. "You'll be fine. If anything he's pretty standoffish, kind of a loner type. Not sure if he's a pervert."

"How do you know him? I forgot to ask him when he stopped by."

"Known the guy and his family since I was a kid. He used to own a cattle ranch not too far from me. Good guy."

She pictured the handsome man. Definitely did not seem strapped for cash. "Why would he work for me? Does he need the money?"

Once again Tobias laughed. "Hell no. He's well off. But he's the sort to get bored and for the last year has been living in a small place. Sold his ranch and misses it. Just won't admit it."

"So, I don't understand. Why not buy a ranch outright? He can save himself the trouble of working here."

"He's the kind that wants to get to know the land. Anyway, I think this will be good for him."

"Right. Okay. Thank you."

"Yeah. Talk at ya later."

For some reason, she narrowed her eyes at the phone. Either Tobias was leaving something out, or she'd grown overly cynical since her break-up.

Of course, desperation meant she'd put up with a housemate for a month. Heck, at least he was hunky. Maybe she'd get lucky and catch glimpses of him without a shirt on.

She trudged to the bedroom and fell back onto the unmade bed. Was it pathetic to consider going to bed at eight thirty? Although in her defense, it was already dark outside.

Her life was reduced to working dawn to dark, eating something that took little effort, followed by an attempt to watch a show or read but falling asleep before too long.

Other than Lucy, she did meet a few friends in town once a week for lunch and visiting. Leaving the house and hanging out was always a lot of fun.

At first, she'd been so excited about living on such beautiful acreage. The vision of living on a ranch, in her imagination, had been so much better than reality. Only a year after moving there, she'd grown tired of spending day after day alone in the evenings, while her ex played at cattle ranching.

When he wasn't working on the ranch, he'd leave for weeks for cattle auctions and such. It was the "and such" that caused their break up.

It turned out instead of cows he was into a different kind of heifer.

Kennedy sat straight up. "Oh no."

The studio over the garage stored all her ex-boyfriend's crap. There was barely any room to move around in there. She'd either have to move everything and clean it or let Rick Edwards stay in the spare bedroom down the hall from hers. Yeah, that wasn't happening. She didn't know the guy from Adam.

"Shit." She fell back onto the bed. "Great."

Instantly wide-awake, she pictured him. She'd never seen anyone that attractive except for maybe in a movie or magazine. The man was exquisite.

Blowing out a breath, she wondered if perhaps he could bunk at Harvey's. No, they only had a two-bedroom place, the extra bedroom was Meg's sewing room.

"Ugh!" Kennedy rolled to her stomach and pushed her face into the pillow. Tomorrow she'd deal with it. Right now a hot shower was shouting out her name.

"Baaaaah!"

Kennedy shrieked and rolled almost falling out of the bed. Arnold studied her with unblinking eyes.

"Oh no you don't. Outside you go." She stood and tugged the reluctant goat toward the kitchen. "Arnold, I don't have the time or energy to play with you. Let's go."

Finally, after bribing the darn thing with two more carrots, she was able to settle him back onto the patio. This time ensuring the kitchen door was fully closed, she headed to shower and crash for the night.

CHAPTER FIVE

★

Ever so often, Rick glanced at his cell phone and considered calling Kennedy and canceling. He'd woken with a big case of "not feeling it". Then he remembered, no phone number.

"Shit."

He'd decided to spend another day in Organicville to hopefully find Bruce. He'd been too tired to drive by the guy's aunt's house the night before. Although Rick planned to get up and go idiot hunting during the night, he'd passed out and not woken until sunlight filtered through the crack in the curtains woke him.

Showered and shirtless, he pulled the curtain back to check on his car. It looked fine, which relieved him. He sniffed the air at the aroma of coffee coming from the other room. Coffee sounded like a great idea.

First things first, call his parents and check on his dogs.

The sound of his dad's happy voice made him smile. "They're great. We just went out for a short walk. Now they're watching me drink my coffee."

Thankfully his parents loved the pair of energetic balls of fur.

He'd do a drive by Bruce's aunt's house and her shop again. Then he'd call his sister to ensure Bruce hadn't hightailed it back. It would be like Clara not to tell him if that had happened.

An hour later, Rick spotted the silver Prius just as he headed toward town. It was an easy find since Bruce slowed down beside him and held up a middle finger. A block later, Bruce pulled over and sauntered into his aunt's shop. Okay, so the guy really didn't give a shit.

Something was up. Bruce didn't particularly seem heartbroken over not seeing Clara. Instead of following the guy into the shop, Rick decided he'd do some investigating. If Bruce had been pulling a stunt and had planned to ditch his sister from the get go, then this time he wouldn't just threaten the ass.

The interior of the diner just down the street from Bruce's aunt's shop was clean and it smelled good. Actually, Rick was relieved at the sound of frying and smell of bacon.

A woman with cropped gray hair immediately slid a cup of steaming coffee in front of him as soon as he bellied up to a tall counter. "Hey sugar." She pointed to a hand drawn menu on the wall. "Bacon, eggs, potatoes and toast. That's the special today."

His lips curved and stomach jumped in anticipation. "Sounds perfect."

Other than a man who no doubt was the driver of the big rig that took up the entire side parking lot, the diner was empty.

"Quiet morning?" Rick asked.

The woman, whose nametag read "Sally", laughed. "Only people with sense eat here. The local grass munchers go across the street." She motioned out the window to another eating establishment. Sure enough, *Green Earth Eats*, seemed to be buzzing with customers. And by "buzzing" being the place was tiny, but busy with about ten people.

Sally made a gagging sound. "Who eats that shit?"

Just then two men walked in and sat at the counter. Both were grumbling about the fact their wives were pissed they refused to eat across the street.

Just like with him, Sally instantly popped cups in front of them. "Glad to see you escaped."

Everyone laughed.

"Do you know Bruce Martin?" Rick asked when he was on his second cup of coffee and finishing up the toast. "I'm looking for him."

Sally leaned both elbows on the counter. "Yeah, his aunt owns the shop just up the street. Sells all kinds of ugly shit."

He really liked the lady. Rick laughed. "Why do you live here? You don't seem the kind. Not that I'm not thankful."

"My husband grew up near here." She hooked a thumb toward the kitchen. "He hides in there and cooks." Not exactly an answer, but Rick let it go. He waited for her to give him more info on pansy-ass.

"Bruce is always here on and off. I think he's sweet on a girl that owns the stationary store lately." Sally shook her head. "Paper made out of elephant poop. Tell you, these people are crazy."

When she walked away to greet people settling at a table, Rick put money on the counter, ensuring a big tip and he walked back out to the cold gloom.

Two weeks before Christmas. This was not exactly how he wanted to spend the time.

THE NEXT DAY, he arrived at Kennedy Brooks' ranch bright and early. Dingo and Chuck, his Labs wasted no time dashing toward the goats. Thankfully the animals were penned. Rick ignored the barking knowing the dogs would soon follow him as he headed to the stables.

Sure enough the hounds on his heels, he greeted Harvey, who instantly began getting to know the dogs.

"Today we're checking all the feed shelters. There are six of them scattered about. Need to ensure they are weather safe. No leaks so the feed stays dry…"

The man continued to tell him what the plan was for the day. He stopped listening when spotting Kennedy heading towards them. She'd come from behind the stables, obviously working on something since she was taking gloves off.

When she looked up, their gazes met. She looked away first. No smile, she came to stand beside Harvey. "Good morning."

Harvey tugged at a horses lead. "Why don't you go get your stuff settled while I let these guys out?"

The rooms over the garage turned out to be much nicer than Rick expected. It was a nice studio apartment built to house one or two people comfortably.

Kennedy kept her distance, but at the same time seemed friendly enough. "I stocked it with fresh linens and towels. There's a washer and dryer in the garage below, you're welcome to use."

He couldn't help but notice how well her form fitting jeans cupped her butt as she went to the small kitchenette. "…coffee maker, microwave…" she rattled off what all was there. He'd have to grab a few groceries. Had only thought to get dog food and dog bowls.

"Can we sit down and talk business tonight? I'll have to go to town and grab a bite, but afterwards…"

"I'll cook something," Kennedy interjected. "I'll have some figures ready and we can talk about what we each expect." Her gaze lingered on his face and at the slight coloring of her cheeks, Rick almost smiled.

So she did find him a bit attractive.

BUSY DAYS ALWAYS went fast, this one was no exception. Before he knew it, it was dark. After feeding the dogs and settling them in the studio, Rick showered, threw on a clean t-shirt, jeans and a thick jacket, he went from his side door to the front of Kennedy's house. She called out for him to enter.

The house looked like something out of one of those shows on television. Although the décor was mostly in subtle tones of whites and grays, it was not sterile in the least. The furniture looked comfortable. The table in the eating area was an old refinished farm table with mix-matched chairs, that were also all painted white.

The room smelled of Italian herbs.

Kennedy stood behind the kitchen island mixing a salad. Next to her was the baby goat. The critter was munching out of a huge bowl of what looked to be cabbage and carrots.

She followed his line of vision. "I am not sure what I'm going to do when he grows up. He gets upset when I put him out."

Rick eyed the goat that looked up seeming to challenge him to say anything negative. "Looks to be quite at home."

"Can you pour the wine please?" Kennedy motioned to a bottle on the counter with her head. "The glasses are right above in the cabinet."

After she put Arnold out, they sat down to plates of lasagna, salad, garlic bread and wine. The meal looked and smelled delicious, and Rick wondered why she'd gone to so much trouble.

It almost felt like a dinner date.

CHAPTER SIX

★

THE GUY WAS too hot for words. It was hard for Kennedy to concentrate on eating.

"Mind if I grab seconds?" he asked and upon her nod, he stood. All six foot something of good-looking went to the kitchen and she watched as much as possible when his back was turned.

"How old are you?" Hopefully the question came across as friendly curiosity.

His dark eyes met hers for a beat as he settled back into the chair across from her. "Forty-one, about to turn forty-two next month, actually. Why do you ask?"

Interesting. "Just curious. Being that you're thinking of buying, wondered how much experience you've got in ranching." Hopefully it was a good reply.

Rick shrugged. "Had a ranch for about fifteen years. Kinda miss it." His brows lowered. "What do you plan to do when you sell?"

The question was one she'd spent a lot of time considering the night before. "I don't want to leave this area, my best friend lives here. Plus my parents are not too far either. I'll probably buy a house with much less land, but enough for Arnold to have some outdoor space."

"Taking the goat, huh? What about the two cows out there?"

It was hard to think of someone mistreating Sandra and Julia. "I am torn. I don't want to take them, but I doubt anyone will want to keep two cows as pets, three actually, if you count the baby."

"The calf," he corrected with a crooked grin.

"Right. The calf."

They discussed the business aspects and decided Rick would work there for a month or until everything was done. She offered to go with him on horseback to tour the perimeter of the land and explain its aspects but he declined.

"I'd rather do this alone. It's one of those things, gotta see if I feel the tug."

It made sense to her. If he didn't bond with the land, it was useless to purchase it. "As long as you let me know as soon as you decide. I'm not in a big hurry to sell, expected to hire a realtor in the spring. Right now, I don't have a place to move to."

He followed her into the kitchen with his dishes, and silently cleaned off his plate and placed it along with his silverware into the dishwasher. The close proximity made Kennedy uneasy. Not because she didn't like it, but because she liked it too much.

The guy had to leave, because if he stayed much longer, she wasn't sure it would be possible to keep from asking him out.

And then why not?

His gaze moved to hers, it was almost as if he read her

thoughts by the darkening of the normally light blue eyes. "So, you're single right now?"

She knew her eyebrows lifted. "Yes. I am. You?" Were they really entering that song and dance? The one where two people tried to assess possibilities?

"Yep."

Not sure what to say, she took a step around him to get her wine glass. His hand on her lower arm stopped Kennedy's progress.

"I know this is fast, but would you be interested in going out sometime?"

And in typical Kennedy fashion, her mouth fell open. Yep, not exactly a good impression. "Ummm…" She was a master of words all of a sudden.

Rick held both hands up. "Hey if you're not interested, no hard feelings." He leaned close to her ear. "But, I would like to explore the possibilities."

Whoa, so he was definitely bold.

"I'd…I think it would be nice to do something." Wow, she was totally screwing this up. "I mean, yes, I'm interested too."

His lips curved and it was impossible to look away. How she wished to be bold enough to kiss him in that moment. Because she knew she'd spend the rest of the night wondering what they would feel like over hers.

What the hell. Kennedy cupped his jaw with her right hand and guided him down closer. "I am very interested in exploring the possibilities." *Heck yeah, now she was talking.*

His mouth was perfect as it covered hers. She held on to his shoulders, head tilted back, lips parting as his tongue dove past her lips. It was not a chaste kiss, it was a perfect first kiss. The man definitely knew what he was doing as his hand held her around the waist ensuring to keep just the right amount of distance from the waist down, while holding her against his chest.

His lips trailed to the corner of her mouth before he straightened and smiled. "Thank you for dinner."

And then he was gone.

Okay so he didn't just turn and make a grand exit. They talked a bit more as he drained his glass of wine and placed it on the counter. She walked him to the door and once again he pressed a kiss to her lips. This time more of a promise of what was to come. But damn if she could remember anything said or could think straight after that first kiss.

"WE KISSED. I can't believe it," Kennedy blurted out to Lucy the next day.

Lucy hurried to the dining room table and dropped her tote. It fell sideways, her notebooks and planner sliding across the surface. "What happened? Who'd you kiss?" Lucy held up both hands. "Don't tell me you and that hunky guy Rick already hooked up?"

In typical Lucy fashion, her friend wiggled in an attempt to do some sort of sexy dance, which reminded Kennedy more of a snake. "You are such a slut." Her friend threw her head back and laughed. "I would've tapped that too, if I were single."

"No. I didn't tap anything. We had dinner and kissed. That's it."

"Oh." Lucy shrugged looking disappointed. "Maybe next time kiddo."

It was hard to put thoughts into words, so Kennedy stirred creamer into her tea and then poured coffee into another cup for Lucy.

"It's too fast. I practically just met the guy. But he asked me out…and well…"

"Whoa," Lucy shook her head, brows drawing together. "There is nothing wrong with being proactive. You like something, go after it. Besides, if you're both single, what the heck. I'm proud of you Ken. You're always regretting not taking action. This time you did it."

"But with him working here and also a prospective buyer…." She left the rest unsaid. Of course, she considered he'd only come on to her in hopes he'd get a better deal on the ranch. Or worse that he was some sort of con.

"Besides, I'm almost thirty-three, I want to get married and have a kid before it's too late. This guy seemed more like the hit and run type."

Lucy went around her and poured creamer into her coffee. "Yes he does, but damn, he can get away with it. So how was the kiss?"

They worked for several hours and one by one, Lucy dispelled all of Kennedy's misgivings about going out with Rick. Worse came to worst, they could always part as friends. No matter what happened between them, she would keep the business aspect of their relationship separate.

Her phone jingled just as Lucy left. She answered it while pushing Arnold out the door.

"Hey. We need to talk. Can I stop by? I'm in the area."

Kennedy let out a long sigh at her ex's voice. "There's nothing to talk about."

"You and I, we have some unfinished business. I'm coming by. Just listen to me alright?"

When he ended the call without waiting for her to answer, she swore out loud. Rick walked in her direction, his dogs on each side running in circles in attempts to get his attention. He'd not spotted her, so she moved back and watched.

Laughing and saying something she could not hear, he pretended to chase after one of the dogs. The delighted dog barked and dashed away, while the other lowered to the ground, his rear in the air in a playful stance waiting his turn to be chased.

The man was a delight to watch. Lean and muscular, she couldn't even begin to imagine what he looked like bereft of clothing. Yeah, that was one place she didn't need to go, especially not with Steve heading there.

Suddenly Arnold dashed toward where Rick and the dogs were. Kennedy held her breath, terrified the dogs would attack the much smaller goat.

"Arnold!" she called out and Rick looked up just as the little goat joined the melee. Arnold hopped in circles and at first the dogs stopped and studied the goat, who continued playing. Just as Kennedy reached them, the dogs sniffed at Arnold. They seemed to accept him, as they began a game of chase and dodge.

"They're pretty friendly," Rick told her with a grin. "Seems they like him."

Arnold dashed around her legs with the dogs in pursuit. Kennedy lifted her arms as they circled her and then ran towards the corrals.

"How are you doing?" Rick neared. "Good day?"

Kennedy nodded. "Productive yes. You?"

His gaze moved over her face and of course her cheeks heated. "Mine was good. Got a good lay of the land. Nice acreage you've got."

She wasn't sure if it was meant as a double entendre. "Thanks. It is beautiful."

"About our date. Want to suggest a place?" Just then Rick turned toward the ranch entrance.

Kennedy's stomach sank. Shit. Her ex was there. Talk about horrible timing. "Let's talk about it later, I best go see who this is." She turned away and hurried toward the front of the house hoping to get Steve indoors before he did or said something stupid.

CHAPTER SEVEN

✪

STEVE WAS TALL, slender and very attractive. For the entire time they'd been together, she'd never once considered seeing anyone else, as he appealed to every part of her. Now after not seeing him for weeks, it was so very different.

The wall she'd built was as tangible as the air entering and leaving her lungs in rapid succession. Not sure why, she glanced from the porch to where Rick continued to stand. Although he didn't look in their direction but instead was bent paying attention to his dogs, she had the impression he watched.

"Come inside." Kennedy took a step back when Steve reached for her, both arms outstretched.

That was so not happening. Kennedy turned away.

His gaze slid towards Rick and for a few moments the men sized each other up. Steve was the first to look away and studied her face. "He seems protective. You dating already?"

"Whether I am or not is none of your business."

Kennedy groaned out loud when once again he looked toward Rick, brows lowered. "Looks familiar."

"What do you want?" She finally managed to get him to

follow her inside. She didn't close the door, nor did she sit. Instead feet planted apart, she crossed her arms and lifted a brow. "You don't have anything left here. Harvey said he took your stuff to your mom's place."

Steve focused past her on the Christmas tree she and Lucy had decorated just the day before. It was the same tree she put up every year. However instead of the usual green and red decorations she and Steve had purchased together, the tree was decorated in white. One less reminder of their life together.

As if understanding, he lowered his gaze for a moment before meeting hers. "I want to come home. I love you Kennedy. I made a horrible mistake."

Was there an apology anywhere in there? Did she miss him asking for forgiveness? He'd cheated on her.

"No."

Once again he reached for her. When she stiffened, he pressed his palm on her upper arm just for second. "I'm sorry. I messed up big time. Tell me what I can do to make things right."

Always a self-assured, cocky guy, it was strange to see so much vulnerability in him when he once again met her gaze. When his lips trembled, Kennedy swallowed, her throat constricting at the uncharacteristic show of emotion. And yet, her heart never once faltered.

"I can't Steve. It's over. I don't feel the same anymore. Maybe it was meant to be. A way for me to realize I am not in love with you. We need to move on."

"Is it him?" The question was loud, forceful. "Is that why you're not even taking the time to think about it?"

Here was the guy she knew. Not going to take no for an answer easily. "It's me. I am moving on. You should too."

"Damn it Kennedy. We have ten years. It should count for something…"

"Did it count when you were fucking around?" she yelled, unable to keep the anger from her voice. "I bet you didn't consider it when you cheated on me."

"It was stupid of me. I don't know why I did it. Can we please try again? I promise…"

Kennedy held up her hand and took a step backward. Why was she still listening to him? Her shield cracked when pictures of them together began forming in her mind. Seeming to know he was gaining ground, Steve took a step toward her. "Please Kennedy. I love you."

Shaking her head, she swiped at a tear that rolled down her cheek. "Please leave."

"Listen to me. Let's have dinner."

The day she'd found out he cheated had started out great. She and Lucy were shooting pictures just outside the kitchen when her cell had dinged. At first she ignored it, but when it kept chiming, she hurried inside fearful it was some sort of emergency.

The pictures were from one of her ranch hand's girlfriend, who'd gone to the cattle auction with Steve and her boyfriend. The upset woman had happened upon Steve and a blonde kissing and had snapped several pictures of the oblivious couple.

Kennedy had asked her to find out more and later that evening, after Steven called and told her he was heading to bed, she'd gone to the hotel to confront him.

Thinking it was room service, the blonde had answered his room door.

She'd not made a scene, instead turned around and headed back to her car. Steve had chased after her pulling his pants on and making all kinds of excuses of how it had "just happened".

"Get out." Kennedy let out a long breath. "We are never getting back together."

"Kennedy…"

"You heard her." The familiar voice behind Steve made him jerk around.

Harvey's steel blue eyes met Steve's. "Go on now. I don't want this to get ugly. She's asked you to leave. I suggest you do."

Although Harvey was older than Steve, he was built and was definitely intimidating in a quiet, I'll kick your ass without breaking a sweat, kinda way.

"Come on Harvey. You know me. I am trying here."

Moving his head side-to-side, Harvey left no room for arguments. Just then one of Rick's dog burst into the room. With happy yelps, he circled Steve's legs demanding attention.

Kennedy almost laughed at Steve's confused expression. When the second dog entered and rushed to the water bowl in the kitchen, she almost groaned.

If the owner appeared next, she'd scream. There were too many men in her presence. Could things grow more awkward?

Steve narrowed his eyes. "What's going on with you?"

Unable help it, she closed her eyes and screamed, "Get out!"

Harvey motioned for Steve to leave, his stern expression giving no room for argument.

Just as Steve reached the door, Rick appeared.

"Are the dogs in here?"

"Who the fuck are you?" Steve's jaw tightened, his lips pressed into a thin line.

Rick didn't bother replying, instead he whistled and the dogs rushed to him.

Without looking at her, he turned on his heel and left.

Great. Just fucking great.

CHAPTER EIGHT

✮

Rick had purposely sent the dogs to the house after hearing the voices grow louder. The sneaky suspicion the guy was Kennedy's ex had unsettled him more than he'd ever want to admit.

All they'd shared was a kiss, nothing more. Besides, he had other issues to deal with. His sister's runaway groom was still…running and before Christmas, come hell or high water, the guy was going to be married to Clara.

Kennedy's ex was almost his height, although Rick had about twenty pounds on him, it didn't mean anything.

Rick stood beside the porch in case Harvey needed him. "Everything all right?"

"I got it handled," Harvey murmured. "Steve was just leaving."

Steve. Okay, so that was the guy's name.

Moments later the car sped away, a trail of dust in its wake. Rick considered if he should check on Kennedy when Harvey walked past toward the stables.

When she came around the corner and stopped short, it

surprised him. Her mottled face, a clear indicator she fought to keep from crying, made his chest constrict.

It tightened all right when he opened his arms and she rushed to him pressing her face into his shoulder. There was shudder of her body followed by a warm wetness on his shirt. Kennedy was crying.

The bastard had made her cry. He should've punched the arrogant guy's face in.

"Hey want to come up to my place? We can watch Netflix and chill."

His attempt at humor had the right effect. She let out a sigh and looked up at him, her lips curving. "I'm sorry to be such a mess. I wish Lucy was here."

"I can eat ice cream and bitch. You got any?" He took her hand and led her back to her front door. After instructing the dogs to settle on the porch, they went inside.

IN HIS FORTY-SOME years of life, he'd never become accustomed to women crying and needing comfort. It seemed no matter what a guy did, they would either keep crying or act as if he was a complete moron.

Kennedy did neither. She brushed tears away and went to the refrigerator. With a quart of chocolate ice cream in one hand, she opened a drawer and pulled out two spoons. She put the items on the kitchen table and plopped down in a chair.

"So much for our first date."

He wasn't sure what she meant. Did this mean she considered this a date? Or did she want to cancel the date they'd not gone on yet. Shit, he hated not knowing what to say.

"This isn't a date. It's me listening to you complain. A date consists of you prettying up and trying to impress me."

Kennedy rolled her eyes and her lips twitched. "You still want to go out with me?"

He leaned forward and ate the ice cream from her spoon. "Hell yeah."

Kennedy's gaze moved to his mouth and her cheeks flushed. "Oh."

Once again he was lost in translation. He dipped his spoon into the ice cream. Not a fan of chocolate, he ate the small amount and put his spoon down. "Unless you're having second thoughts about him."

Fuck. What was he doing? This was not a made for TV movie. In his experience, this was the perfect time to take advantage of her moment of weakness. Pounce on the opportunity. It was perfect timing to get her in bed. At the direction of his thoughts, Rick grimaced. He was an idiot.

"I want to sleep with you."

Her blunt comment made his eyes round. Had she read his mind? Damn, he shifted in his chair. Okay so he had a hard-on, but she couldn't see it through the table.

Cupping the back of her head, he pulled her forward and covered her mouth with his. The kiss, meant to be soft, went a bit too long, but he managed to drag himself back. "This is not a good time. You're upset and probably not thinking clearly."

Kennedy nodded. "This is embarrassing. Forget I said anything."

"Nope, don't be embarrassed. I want to sleep with you too. I tell you what. Think about it and if you still want to be with me, you know where I live." He pressed another kiss to her lips, this time taking her mouth fully to convey how much he wanted to see her again.

Somehow he managed to stand and hopefully keep his hard-on hidden as he walked out.

HAD HE BEEN an idiot to turn her down? Would the opportunity present itself again? Was he a complete moron?

An hour later, the knock at his door answered the question.

Okay so the last one was still up in the air. But when he opened the door to the beautiful woman, he forgot all about vulnerability, the quest for the elusive groom, and even Christmas.

Damn she was gorgeous.

"I brought wine." Kennedy held up a bottle. "Got glasses?"

Rick smiled. "Yep, I think so." He motioned for her to enter.

When they reached the small kitchenette, she put the bottle down on the counter and looked up at him.

They were so not going to drink any wine.

ALTHOUGH KENNEDY EXPECTED sex with Rick to be off the charts, what she wasn't prepared for was the strength of the jolt at his first touch. He came up behind her as she placed the wine down. Pulling her back against him, he slid a hand down the front of her jeans. Heated breath and the trail of his tongue down the side of her neck were enough to almost finish her off.

She threw her head back and gasped when his fingers delved between her folds. Need grew exponentially. Urgency and want blurred together. Kennedy wanted to prolong this portion, the foreplay between them, as long as possible.

By the huge bulge pressing against her butt, the man was well endowed. She pushed back gratified at the low moan in her ear.

His teeth grazed over the sensitive area just below her ear and Kennedy turned her head so he could take her mouth with his.

With his free hand, Rick took Kennedy's jawline holding her in place and pushed his tongue past her parted lips. Damn it how she wanted another part of him in her mouth.

It wouldn't do to wait, no matter how much she fought the urge to prolong the moment, when his fingers moved to her most sensitive part, she shuddered and cried out.

Her legs shook and her knees threatened to buckle. Thankfully Rick scooped her up and carried her to the small bedroom, closing the door with his foot.

Snow began falling outside, the flakes falling against the glass panes. Absently, Kennedy wondered if she'd remember the fact later.

In between kisses and caresses, they undressed, clothing strewn all over the room in their hurry.

The man was built like a dream. Outside of daydreams, she didn't remember ever seeing someone so hunky. Definitely not in person. Although Steve was in good shape, no one she'd been with compared to Rick.

His lips curved as if reading her mind. "I don't have much to do, so I spend a lot of time working out. By the way you're looking, it was worth it."

Like a predator, he stalked closer. "Yeah, definitely worth every damn minute."

Kennedy kneeled on the floor. "Come closer."

Although his eyes narrowed, as if unsure, he did as she requested and Kennedy chuckled. "I won't hurt you, I promise."

"That's not what I'm afraid of." He didn't elaborate and although she wanted to ask, her attention was taken when Rick leaned forward, cupped her face and took her mouth with hunger.

The man knew how to kiss, his lips traveling over hers as he sucked her bottom lip while his tongue outlined the upper. He nipped at the corners of her mouth ensuring to pay attention to every inch.

"Rick," Kennedy gasped out this name looking up at him. She took his length in hand and stroked him. The skin was soft, silky almost over the hardness, the contradiction a total turn-on. She hoped he was prepared, because she'd not wanted someone this bad in so long.

He bucked into her hand, a low groan escaping. When she bent forward and licked the underside of him and then pulled the head of his cock into her mouth, Rick stiffened. "Augh."

He took her hair and held her steady and slowly slid deeper into her mouth until she gagged. Kennedy relaxed her throat. Rick pulled back and then surged back into her mouth until hitting her throat. She held on to his thighs allowing him to make love to her mouth.

Definitely a new experience for her and the most sensual encounter ever.

His hips moved forward and she took inch after inch until his breathing became ragged.

"The bed now." Rick lifting her into his arms and rushing toward the bed followed his guttural command.

CHAPTER NINE

★

THE MUSTANG STOOD out in the small dirt and snow covered parking lot filled with vintage Beetles, Prius' and other cars too ugly to take inventory of.

Rick climbed out and adjusted his baseball cap to keep the sun off his eyes. Although he wore sunglasses, the high sun reflecting off the bit of snow made it hard to see, so he'd reached for the ball cap.

First he looked toward Bruce's aunt's store, but then decided to go to the stationary place first.

The smell of patchouli outside the store reminded him of younger days. Chimes jingled overhead and he pushed beads out of the way to enter the shop.

A pretty blonde with braids greeted him with a wave. She wore what looked to be about twenty bracelets on each wrist and colorful rings on every finger. "Good morning," she said studying him. "How can I help you?"

"Looking for Bruce."

Her brows lowered. "He's not here." Her gaze moved past him to the street. "I helped him make a beautiful gift for his fiancée. I bet he's gone back there to give it to her."

A gift? Rick looked around the small shop not finding anything remotely interesting. Definitely nothing his sister, who preferred classically cut clothes and conservative pearls, would wear.

"Interesting. Can you tell me what he made?"

The blonde shrugged. "I suppose it doesn't hurt to show you." She went to the back wall to a dusty glass display case and Rick followed.

"Something like this. Except, he wrapped the wire around a beautiful miniature gold toy soldier, to commemorate their first date. He said they went to see The Nutcracker."

Displayed on black velvet were pairs of intricate gold wire earrings, necklaces and matching bracelets. The wire was wrapped delicately around different colored crystals and stones of various sizes. One stone, a soft white loose stone nestled in a nest of black velvet got his attention. For some reason, it reminded him of Kennedy.

MOMENTS LATER WITH a package in hand, Rick walked out. He felt silly holding the brown bag with brightly colored tissue, so he hurried to the Mustang to deposit it.

Just as he closed the car door, Bruce crossed the street toward his aunt's shop.

If he'd purchased a gift for Clara, why wasn't he taking it to her? It made no sense for him to remain there longer. Perhaps the guy was dumber than Rick thought.

Rick jogged to cut Bruce off just as he reached for the door.

The guy's widened eyes met his and then looked toward where he'd come from.

"Instead of running, why don't you just tell me what you plan to do?" Rick kept his attention on Bruce's hands in case the guy tried to deck him again.

"Why are you still here?" Bruce took a step back and crossed his arms. "You've made your point. You don't want me to marry Clara."

The guy swallowed visibly. "I have made a decision. You can kill me if you want, but I'm going to marry your sister and there isn't a damn thing you can do about it."

There wasn't one sign of vulnerability and Rick couldn't help but wait to see what else the guy had to say.

Bruce swallowed again, a noticeable flush colored his face.

Tapping on the window caught their attention. Bruce's aunt smiled widely and began spraying white onto the glass.

"She's going to try to spell Merry Christmas backwards. Always get's it wrong," Bruce muttered.

"I was wrong for what I did to you." Rick let out a sigh. "I apologize."

"Unfortunately, I'm the coward. I freaked out and ran." Bruce lowered his arms and looked across the street in thought. When he returned his gaze to Rick, his jaw was set. "Look, I'm not all bulked up and big like you, but I'm man enough to stand before you and tell you that I don't care if I have to crawl on my hands and knees and ask Clara to forgive me. I am going to do it. I love your sister."

"She loves you too." Damn if he didn't feel two inches tall. "It was Clara who sent me to bring you back."

Bruce's eyes widened. "Why didn't you say that to begin with?" He glanced toward the parking lot as if calculating how quick he could get to his car.

"You sucker punched me."

"I did, didn't I?" For the first time, Bruce smiled. "Didn't see that comin' did ya?"

Rick shook his head. "No, and I deserved it."

"I'm going back home," Bruce told his aunt, who'd sprayed "Merry" with the "e" backwards. Before Rick could say another word, Bruce was already across the street. Had to give it to the guy, he was fast.

"Hey Bruce," Rick called out and jogged toward where Bruce stood next to his car. "Why didn't you call Clara and explain?"

Bruce let out a huff, his cheeks expanding. "I left my cell there at our place. Plus what the hell would I say? Sorry for being a coward and letting your brother scare me off?"

"Want me to call her?"

"No," Bruce said shaking his head. "I have to do this in person."

As the Prius sped off, Rick remained rooted to the spot. He glanced at his cell before dialing his sister.

"What do you want?" Her voice was hollow at his ear. "You better have good news."

"I'm sorry."

"Yeah, well that's not good enough. You ruined what was supposed to be the best day of my life."

"I'll help you make the wedding even better."

"How the hell are you going to do that?" Her voice pitched

with emotion. "Stop screwing around. Did you find Bruce?"

"Just talked to him. Sis, don't be hard on him. It's my fault."

Clara was silent so Rick continued, "Ever consider a Christmas wedding?"

"No, I didn't. The reason we planned our wedding when we did was because I didn't want our anniversary overshadowed by Christmas."

"A Christmas Eve wedding?"

"No."

"New Years?"

"Hell no."

He was running out of ideas, but was enjoying that through the banter, she sounded more like her usual self.

"The twenty-sixth. The day after would be good."

"Everyone will be too tired to come."

"Shit Clara, the twenty-second then."

"That's in a week. We can't put together a wedding in a week." He thought he heard a chuckle. "Just face the facts, I won't get married this year. You ruined it and now you have to live with it. I'm hanging up on you now."

The blonde from the shop ambled across the street toward the ugly clothes boutique and walked in. Rick jogged back to the shop and entered.

Bruce's aunt was in spray paint heaven, can in hand, she turned to him with a smile. Upon recognizing him, she frowned. "Oh, you're still here."

With raised eyebrows, the blonde looked between them. "Is he a bad guy?"

Good grief, where the hell were these people from? Mars?

"I wanted to invite you to the wedding. It's going to be on the twenty-second."

Bruce's aunt looked to the blonde as if to confirm what he said before nodding slowly. "Nice choice, on a Thursday, that's unconventional. Where?"

"You want me to do what?" Kennedy stared at him as if he'd grown a horn between his eyes. "A wedding? Here? In six days?"

"I'll help." Lucy, her friend clapped. "How fun. You guys barely did the deed and now you're getting hitched."

Rick's eyes widened and he choked on his own spit. "Ugh…no…"

Relief flooded when Kennedy giggled. "We're not the ones getting married Lucy."

"Oh darn," Lucy frowned and stalked to Rick. "But you are going to marry her. Mark my word. I'm never wrong about these things."

Not sure what to say, Rick cleared his throat and looked to Kennedy for help. She shrugged and rolled her eyes. Damn if she didn't look enticing in her weathered jeans and tight sweater. He took a moment to look her over before realizing Lucy stared up at him. "We'll see."

"That's what people say when they're indecisive," Lucy replied obviously not liking his answer. "But anyways. Wedding?"

"What if you go through all the work and expense and your sister says no?" Kennedy, the reasonable one of the three, pointed out. "It takes a lot of work to pull something like this together."

"I'll have to take the chance." Rick walked to the large picture window and peered out toward the stables. "When we were kids, Clara always talked about a barn wedding. She hated that her horse could not attend a regular wedding."

"Horses are invited?" Lucy lifted her cup and met his gaze. "Awesome."

CHAPTER TEN

Clara

She couldn't just accept him back. Although every part of her being screamed for her to allow Bruce back into her life, he'd hurt her deeply.

As much as she blamed her brother for ruining the wedding, it was Bruce who'd made the decision to not show up. He'd left her alone on the most important day of their relationship.

For the third day, flowers arrived joining the now overflowing collection that included stuffed animals, balloons, and fruit baskets. If he kept it up, she would be able to open a shop of her own.

He'd come to her doorstep several times a day and she'd yet to open the door. Each time, she'd cried afterwards, not sure what to do.

"My God." Her mother walked in, letting herself in with her key. "He is really going overboard."

"Not enough to make me reconsider marrying him. I thought I wanted to, but what if anytime we face something hard, he runs?"

"That's a valid question." Her mother went to the kitchen and pushed a fruit basket out of the way to reach the coffee maker. "But we both know you and Bruce are the once-in-a-lifetime kind of thing. You have loved each other since elementary school."

"He left me standing at the alter. He didn't show up." A tear slid down her face and she swiped it away. "He's a butthead."

"That he is," her mother agreed. "Got any creamer?"

"Mom! Why are you acting as if it's nothing to get stuck with a twenty-thousand dollar wedding bill?"

"There it is." Her mother reached for the creamer and stirred it into her cup. "Honey, the money is spent. Besides, Bruce already paid us back. He sent apology flowers to us too. The flower shop must love him."

Clara wanted to choke her mother. "Why didn't you tell me? He did?"

"You've got enough on your mind." Her mother waved at the flowers. "Let him stew a couple more days. Then take him back."

Sinking into a chair, she was glad when her mother began boiling water for tea. "You know, I hate living here alone. I miss him so much."

"Rick told me you nixed a New Year's Eve wedding."

Sarah wished she had magical powers. She'd appear wherever Rick was and slap him. Just for the heck of it. "Yes. Besides, why should I have to go through all the trouble to plan another wedding? If anything, Rick should be doing it. Although, I'd be terrified of what he'd come up with."

"A cow and Mustang theme would be my guess," her mother

said with a chuckle, and Clara couldn't help but smile.

"I don't think I'd look good in a camouflage dress."

Her heart skipped when the doorbell rang. "More flowers?"

"I'll get it," her mother exclaimed. "Maybe it's one of those cut up fruit baskets. I'd love that."

"Mom, it isn't not a game." Clara gave up trying to stop her mother and instead sipped her tea not bothering to see what size this bouquet would be.

For a moment it was silent, then soft voices could be heard as her mother accepted whatever it was and signed for it. Goodness, how much more would be delivered? She'd already decided to load some into her truck and deliver them to the old folk's home nearby. Maybe she'd drop some off to the clinic and her church too.

"Clara." Bruce's voice made her spit out her tea and cough. "Your Mom let me in."

Unable to do more than breathe, Clara struggled not to cry. Her first reaction was to kick him out, the second was to throw her arms around him. Instead, she stared straight ahead until a bouquet of roses was lowered in front of her.

"More flowers?"

He snatched them back.

"I don't know what else to do? I did send your favorite pizza the other day."

She'd eaten it with gusto, thinking her parents had sent it. "You did?"

"And I also sent a box of butterflies, but then I realized you were out of town and came over to rescue them. I let them go. Hope some hung around."

Pressing her lips together not to laugh, she turned to face him.

He held a necklace up. A nutcracker dangled from a dainty chain. "I made this for you."

Her handsome Bruce. With a five o'clock shadow and tussled hair, he looked as handsome as ever. He'd moved back to stand by the kitchen island. The man had good instincts. If the mood wasn't right, she'd beat the shit out of him with the roses he was holding and choke him with the necklace. Okay so she'd not damage the necklace perhaps.

"You didn't show up. How could you do that to me?" Her voice hitched and she set her jaw. "Asshole."

When he took a step forward, she stuck out both hands. "Don't come any closer. I will beat you with the flowers you're holding."

With a thud, Bruce placed the vase on the counter. "I am the worst coward. I let your brother intimidate me. I am willing to do anything you ask, to convince you to take me back."

"Fine." Clara lifted her chin. "I'm not going to let you walk back out the front door until we come to a decision. Either we'll accept that we'll never get over this, or we'll make up and get married."

He swallowed and nodded. Clara wished she knew what the right answer was. At the moment all she wished for was for it to be Christmas. She'd either be nursing a broken heart, or happily married.

CHAPTER ELEVEN

⭐

Kennedy stretched out her sore arms. Between getting the ranch prepared for the winter and all the decorations and such in the barn, it had been a hard three days. The worst part was Rick had not informed his sister yet.

Just then a tug at her pants leg made her look down. Arnold's unblinking eyes looked up at her.

"I just gave you two carrots young man. You need to go bother your mama." She took the goat by the collar and tugged him to the door.

When she opened the door, two dogs bounded in to Arnold's delight. They raced around the room playing before dashing out. Rick's car pulled up and came to a stop in front of the house and her stomach dipped. They'd not been alone since having sex. Between him going to find the elusive groom and Lucy spending the night, they'd not had time.

He climbed out of the car and went around to the back. Today he was dressed for the cold. Both he and Harvey had spent a lot of time outdoors checking the shelters and delivering the feed they pulled in wagons behind four-wheelers.

"Hi," Rick smiled at her. Even in a thick jacket and a beanie pulled down low, he was a sight. "I brought you something the other day and forgot to give it to you."

He carried a dainty brown paper bag, crumpled colorful tissue stuffed into it.

"It got crushed." Rick held out the bag.

Taking the gift, Kennedy shivered. "Come inside, it's freezing."

Once inside, he seemed to grow larger, his presence overtaking all her senses. His gaze moved from her face to the bag. "Open it."

"Oh." Now she felt like a doofus. "Thank you." She dug out a small purple velvet drawstring bag. Inside of it was a gold chain with a wire-wrapped beautiful pure white stone. She held it up and the light made it sparkle. "Wow. It's amazing." She finally dragged her eyes from it to look at Rick, whose smile was just as breathtaking.

"Where did you find it? I've never seen something so pretty."

He rolled his eyes and shrugged. "It's nothing that great. Just a trinket."

Kennedy ignored him and hurried to a mirror on the wall beside the door. She put the necklace on. The wire-wrapped stone hung just above the center of her breasts. "I love it, thank you so much."

"Not sure why I bought it. It reminded me of you," Rick said coming up behind her and wrapping his arms around her waist. His eyes met hers in the mirror. "I'd like to see you wearing only the necklace. Nothing else."

Her slutty body turned hot and gooey and she leaned her

head back on his shoulder. "Only if you leave that beanie on."

His deep chuckle was like a drug and her brain turned to fog. The plan had been to inform him they could not sleep together again. Her priority was preparing the ranch and selling it, not cavorting with the ranch hand and prospective buyer.

A bright light from outside lit the room. It was followed by dogs barking and Arnold's attempt to do the same. The moment broken, Kennedy took a step away from Rick and went to the door.

It was a dark SUV from which a woman climbed out and smiled broadly. "Rick, we need to talk."

"Hi Mom," Rick said immediately moving away from Kennedy and going to the woman who looked toward her. "I thought you were staying in an apartment."

He glanced at Kennedy. "Mom, this is Kennedy."

The woman smiled at her and walked up the steps. She was slender with the grace of self-assurance. In slacks and a button-up blue blouse, she wore her shoulder length grey-streaked hair straight. On her wrists there were several chunky bracelets that matched the earrings she wore.

Kennedy was glad she'd decided to wear a nice sweater with her jeans that day. Although, she was barefoot and her hair was probably a disheveled mess.

"I had the hardest time finding the place," Rick's mother said bending to pet the dogs that demanded attention. Her eyes widened and she hesitated when Arnold joined in. She glanced up at Kennedy. "Does he know he's a goat?"

Kennedy laughed. "I don't think so. Please come in Mrs. Edwards."

"Call me Janice. I need to talk to Rick if you don't mind. I have to hurry back."

"Of course not. I have things to do in my office. I'll leave you two alone."

"I'm staying in the studio over here." Rick pointed to the side of the house.

His mother dismissed him and walked into the living space. "Very nice home, Kennedy."

ENSCONCED IN HER office, Kennedy absently rubbed the stone around her neck and wondered what Rick and his mother spoke about. It had been painfully obvious he didn't want his mother to suspect anything happened between them by the wide berth he gave Kennedy once his mother arrived.

Although, if she were to be honest, his actions weren't surprising. A one-time fling did not constitute any kind of relationship. Why was she hoping for more?

Probably because Rick was the first man she'd slept with since Steve. Because not only had it been the best sex ever, but also because she'd felt a connection with him.

"Stupid, stupid," Kennedy mumbled and slid her fingers across the laptop pad. The sooner Rick made an offer on the ranch and left, the better. Once this crazy wedding fiasco transpired and the work was done, she'd ask him to leave. She and Harvey could finish preparing for winter. For the moment, she was stuck.

Once his mother left, she'd ensure to keep her distance. Hopefully he'd not push to sleep with her.

When it came to Frederick Edwards, she could not say no.

Two taps were followed by the door opening and Rick peering in. "Thanks for that. Mom wants to be sure everything is ready for Thursday."

"She's nice."

He nodded, his brow furrowed. "I best get on. See you in the morning."

Not waiting for her to reply, he left and Kennedy could only stare at the empty doorway. What exactly happened?

Yes, she'd hoped that he'd not stay, but at the same time, there seemed to be a sort of shift in him. Almost as if his mother being there had spotlighted the fact they had been intimate and he did not like it.

She was making too much of it. Surely it was just that the moment had been lost with his mother's visit.

Just as she went to the front door to fetch Arnold, a ding got her attention. Rick's cell phone was on the coffee table. On the display a text.

Want you naked
See you Saturday.

The display showed "Tina" as the contact just as the phone dimmed. Of course he was seeing other people. This was a good reminder to stand her ground and stay away from him. Her heart was not ready for a casual relationship.

Kennedy shuddered at the idea she'd slept with someone who was obviously sleeping with someone else. The rap at the door made her jump and she took a guilty step back from the cellphone.

"Forgot my phone," Rick said when she opened the door.

Making a show of looking for it, she glanced around the room purposely avoiding looking at both the offending object and Rick. He walked in, picked it up and shoved it into his pocket.

"Thanks." Flashing a crooked grin, he walked back out.

CHAPTER TWELVE

IT WAS TIME to cut and run. If only he'd not planned the wedding, Rick would be packing up and hightailing it out of Dodge.

The woman was starting to get under his skin and now listening to the dogs snoring, he pictured her next to him on the couch as he attempted to watch a documentary on some weird type of shit or another.

He'd definitely decided to not buy the land, but go back to his cabin and stick to the plan of drifting from place to place. Helping friends and maybe working the rodeo for a bit. Do whatever the fuck he wanted.

Owning a ranch was much like marriage. It meant being tied down. It hadn't worked in the past and it wouldn't work again.

So yeah, he looked forward to getting up every morning and getting out there to help out. The smell of the outdoors called to him, almost as much as the mooing of cows and the horses nickering.

One divorce was enough of a lesson that when it came to commitment, he was a failure.

Dingo groaned and rearranged himself not opening his eyes and Rick chuckled. If only he could be as carefree.

He'd lost the mood to head to Kennedy's bed when his mom had showed up. Before his mom got there, they were definitely headed to bed. However, after a few comments from his mother about how suited he and Kennedy seemed, Rick had sobered up and lost any kind of desire to stay the night.

Damn he was an asshole. The combination of sitting alone in the dark and what Bruce, the nerd, had said earlier cemented that shit into his brain.

Kennedy deserved better. After the guy Steve, the last thing she needed was a guy without a life plan.

Hopefully the wedding would be a success. His sister would be happy and things would progress for the family.

His cellphone buzzed.

"Yeah?"

Tobias chuckled. "Don't sound so excited to hear my voice. Not the booty call you were expecting?"

Rick thought back to his text turning down Tina's offer. "Yeah, you're not my type at all."

"My feelings are hurt."

Tobias had prefect timing. A good distraction from his thoughts.

"How are things there? You buying the place?"

Okay, maybe not.

"I don't think so. I'm not sure I want to go back to the grind of ranching and being tied down to land."

There was a beat of silence. "You have to move on man. Look, let me be honest. Your Dad put me up to this. Asked me to find a place for sale and make arrangements for you to work the land and get back to your life. He and the family…they're worried about you. You sit up in the cabin for days without talking to anyone…"

"What the fuck? Did Kennedy know about this?"

"Who? Oh…no…no I didn't tell her. I told her you would probably waffle back and forth and there was a chance you'd not buy it."

In other words, they'd discussed his private life.

His jaw protested his gritted teeth. "What did you tell her about me?"

"Nothing man. Just that I had a friend who might be in the market to buy, but that you were not sure. That's it."

Not sure what to believe, he wanted to cut the conversation short, but Tobias continued. "Look. I'm with your Dad. Ranching is what you were born to do. Although you help out at your family's place, it's just land he piddles around on. It's not a working ranch."

Finally, after a few more "uh huhs" and "yeah, alrights", they ended the conversation. He stared at the phone considering calling his father, then his mother, finally he dialed Clara.

"What?" Her voice, even if curt settled his mind. "Rick?"

"Yeah."

"What's wrong?"

"I don't know."

There was the sound of shuffling and soft voices as she probably told Bruce who called. "Do you need me to come there?"

Leave it to Clara to never hesitate to take action when it came to him. No matter that she was a brat, she took her role as big sister seriously.

"Nah. Just thinking about how fucked up I am. I'm sorry."

She huffed. "You are an asshole, true. But you also have a big heart. What happened?"

"Fuck sis…I am lost as hell. Don't know what to do about it. Can't seem to move on."

"I noticed." The sound of liquid pouring meant she was about to get a glass of wine and get philosophical.

Rick waited not sure what to say, not even positive why he'd called other than knowing Clara always calmed his mind and never steered him wrong. Should have listened when she advised him not to get married the first time.

"So your ex messed you over. But think about it this way, you loved her and that's good. Now we have proof you do have a soul."

He couldn't help the chuckle. "Great."

"Yes. And you're out there at a ranch. Actually out of the damn cabin. So if this entire wedding thing you ruined got you back out and living, then it's worth all of my tears."

Shit now he was blinking some of his own. "No, I was wrong."

"Shut up and listen," Clara snapped. "Whatever you're fighting right now. Stop it. Buy the freakin' ranch. Tell the girl you love her and by the way…whatever you and Mom are planning, it better not include any kind of audience. Because if I know you two, it's going to be embarrassing as hell."

"Good night sis. I love you."

Clara told him what she was drinking and he laughed. Apparently, she'd made it her mission to drink all the wine leftover from the wedding. "Hey," she finally said. "Good night and I'm still mad at you. You still owe me big time."

When they ended the call, he stared at the television screen. An older man wearing glasses seemed excited at pointing out the discovery of some sort of bone fragment. Wow, and he thought he didn't have a life.

CHAPTER THIRTEEN

Clara

"I UNDERSTAND YOU want me to go to the ranch and talk to Rick about buying it. But, this dressing up for it is just plain silly," Clara repeated as she looked through the windshield at the landscape.

"So Bruce is back to work then?" Her mother ignored her complaint. "How are you two doing?"

As a matter of fact, Bruce had not only returned to work, but he seemed rather cheerful about it. Although she understood the geeks at the science research center welcomed him back with open arms, it seemed strange how giddy he'd been that morning about heading back to work. That morning, he'd left especially early, a wild look in his eyes.

"He's back to work and we are doing great. Although, he keeps apologizing for everything." Clara looked to the back seat. "What is that smell?"

Her mother glanced into the rear view mirror. "Probably road kill."

"It smells like flowers. Sweet."

"Oh that. I have one of those potpourri packs under the seat."

Odd. Her mother always preferred fragrances more along the tropical scents. "Well, it smells great."

They pulled into a ranch, just about half an hour from where she and Bruce lived. Immediately she recognized Rick's car. It stood out next to two trucks and a tiny Fiat. Other than the cows in a snowy field to the right and a couple goats running loose, no one seemed to be about.

"They might be out on horseback." Her mother pointed out to a field. "Is that Rick?"

Clara looked, but there wasn't anyone anywhere. She squinted and leaned forward and peered out the passenger window. "I don't see anyone."

"Over there," her mother said, pointing again to the empty field. "On the right."

"I don't see anyone." She scanned the area slowly. "Either I'm going blind, or you have eagle eyes."

Her chuckle stuck in her throat when they pulled up to a barn. On both sides of the doors stood two men dressed in some sort of British soldier costume.

Clara frowned. "What are they doing?"

"Beats me," her mother replied, studying the men. "Come on, let's investigate."

When they climbed out, Clara pulled her coat on tighter. Wearing a dress was such a silly idea. Her Mom was up to something, but she couldn't put her finger on it. If it was a scheme to get Rick to propose to the lady, Kennedy, or something of the sort, they were about to fail.

"Oh wait," her mother called out. "I have something in the trunk." Clara followed her mom keeping an eye on the men who stood very still. She waved at them, but neither waved back. One did give a subtle nod.

Her mother produced what looked to be a bouquet. In the mixture of pink and white flowers rose gold glittery stems twisted into a swirl. "How beautiful," Clara exclaimed, almost forgetting the British soldiers.

"Hold it for me. I have another thing to carry." Her mother dug out a white cloak and held it.

They walked toward the barn. At the doorway, one of the soldiers reached for her coat.

Perplexed Clara allowed him to remove it, while the other held the flowers. Her eyes popped wide upon stepping past a curtain, the music to the Nutcracker Suite filled the air and her mother placed the plush thick cloak on her shoulders.

"It's your wedding honey," her mother whispered.

The barn was a fantasy of white-flocked Christmas trees and sparkling lights hanging from the ceiling. Clara's gaze flew from a group of women dressed in ballerina costumes to the huge tree at the front of the space.

When the March from the Nutcracker ballet played, familiar people, who'd been at her disastrous wedding, walked in from rear entries and ignoring her they silently went to seats. It was as if she were invisible as they took seats.

The ballerina's came to life as the familiar Dance of the Sugar Plum Fairy played over speakers. Clara had not closed her mouth yet.

Bruce, Rick, nor her father were anywhere in sight. Strange

wedding.

The ballerinas continued their dance in front of where the people were seated and when the music faded, they lined up side-by-side.

The music changed to the waltz and just as her father and Rick flanked her. Her father dressed in costume, cut a fine figure. Rick was also dressed in period costume and Clara gasped at how handsome he looked. His grin told her that the rascal knew it.

Her father took her left arm as she moved the bouquet to her right. When she looked up to the front again, not only had a clergy appeared, but also Bruce, dressed in the Prince's costume of a blue top and white slacks.

Her heart fluttered and tears slid down both cheeks as she stopped trying to hold them back.

With her brother on the opposite side, she walked down the center of the room toward Bruce.

Through hazy eyes, she noted every guest was dressed in a period costume and some women even donned wigs. Fans fluttered in sync to the music as the soldiers stood side by side along the walls in between the trees. The ballerinas floated back down the sides of the barn leaving her with the two men.

"Who gives this woman?" the clergy's voice rang out and both Rick and her father answered that they did.

Her father guided her to stand beside Bruce whose eyes also sparkled with moisture.

Rick stood behind Bruce and beside her was her best friend Emily, who looked beautiful in powder pink ballet style dress.

She smiled brightly with tears falling down her cheeks. "Surprise," Emily whispered.

It was the wedding of her dreams. So much more beautiful than anything any woman could imagine. At her age, she assumed it was best to have a simple "elegant" affair. But this was definitely a dream come true.

While the vows were exchanged, soft classical music played so low it was barely audible.

Afterward, elegantly dressed servers treated guests to champagne and appetizers. And tables loaded with elegant silver dishes were rolled in. Clara could not stop gasping as she noticed detail after detail.

The guests did the same, exploring every detail of the space. Tables had been set out with beautiful wooden nutcrackers at every setting for the guests to take home along with what looked to be boxes of sweets.

"How did you get all this done is so little time?" Clara asked her brother who approached with a woman beside him.

His gaze moved to the beautiful brunette. "Kennedy and her friend Lucy did most of the work."

Kennedy shrugged. "Actually Lucy has a friend that works with Billings Ballet and they graciously allowed for all the props to be borrowed. Some of the cast is here as well. They were excited to participate."

"Oh my goodness. They are so beautiful. Everything is so perfect. I don't know what to say. I'm speechless."

"I owed you." Rick looked around the room. "It's cool."

Leave it to her brother to make light of the huge gesture.

"It's more than cool." Clara kissed his cheek.

Bruce came up beside her and looked to Rick. "Your brother outdid himself."

"Yes," Clara sighed happily. "He did. You all did."

CHAPTER FOURTEEN

⭐

KENNEDY WOKE TO the sound of dogs barking and Arnold's attempt at sounding like them. She sat straight up thinking they were in the house, but on further inspection realized they were outside her bedroom window. Somehow the dogs had gotten the gate to her flower garden open and were running in circles with the goat.

She blinked into the sunlight as Neo and Trinity joined the fun. Great, now they got even noisier.

The alarm clock displayed seven in the morning. "Damn it," she groaned falling back into the pillows. The goats were mischievous, but the dogs were instigators.

Moments later a deep voice permeated her foggy brain. "Get out of there. Dingo. Chuck. Come."

"Come!" Rick called louder as he neared her window. "Shit. Stop."

Kennedy giggled wondering what was happening. No doubt, not only the dogs, but also the goats had rushed Rick in hopes of getting treats.

"Stop," he said again. Unable to help it, she slid from the

bed and went to the window.

Just outside the garden gate, Rick was surrounded by goats and dogs. The animals nudged each other aside to jump on him or nuzzle his pockets. When he pushed one face away, another would take its place.

Kennedy began laughing unable to keep her voice down. Rick looked to the window, but continued frowning.

Finally, she took pity on him. She dragged sweats over her pajama shorts and headed to the kitchen side door. From a hook beside the door, she shrugged on a jacket and slipped her feet into boots.

The cold air made her gasp as she trudged to the side of the house. "Arnold."

She held up three carrots she'd grabbed from the kitchen and wiggled them in the air. The goats hurried toward her. Along the way, Morpheus appeared and joined them.

Breaking the carrots into pieces, she fed the goats as Rick called out, "Thanks." Both he and the dogs disappeared from view.

Back inside, Kennedy shivered and went to the thermostat. It read seventy-four, but it felt colder. The fireplace would help warm up the living space.

Once the hearth glowed with a fire from the gas line, she let out a contented sigh.

Not normally an early riser, she decided to take advantage and have a relaxing morning. Read, tea…something. She looked to the front door. Perhaps invite Rick for breakfast.

"No," she said out loud. Rick had asked to speak to her later this day. Kennedy was sure he intended to give her the key to the studio and inform her he'd not be purchasing the ranch.

BY THAT AFTERNOON, Kennedy had run out of things to do. The kitchen was clean, her bed linens changed, and dirty ones washed. She paced and looked outside as rain began falling.

She peered into the pantry with little interest. Oatmeal, raisins…

Moments later, she slid a tray of cookies into the oven.

When she was placing the hot cookies onto a plate, a rap at her door made her stomach flip. It was probably him.

Purposely in the same sweat pants from earlier that morning and a hoody, Kennedy was comfortable that he'd not think she'd been waiting for him. Instead of shoes, she wore fuzzy slippers and her hair was pulled up into a messy bun.

He not only stood in the doorway, he filled the space. Darkened blue eyes met hers with so much intensity, Kennedy took a step backward.

After motioning him to enter, she turned and hurried to the safety of the kitchen. There was too much temptation in the room and the barrier of the kitchen's island would help. Not much, but it was better than nothing.

He carried some papers and a crumpled bag. "I brought the paperwork I got from my lawyer, figured we'd go over it." Rick placed it on the kitchen table but didn't sit.

"Let me get this second batch of cookies out. Would you like coffee?"

"We need to talk." He circled the island closing the distance between them. "I owe you an explanation. I know things were left unfinished."

Kennedy ignored the pang in her chest. The words, the fact he was about to explain his departure, should not matter so much.

They'd barely gotten to know one another. And yet over the last week, spending time daily on the wedding plans did bring them closer as friends. A friendship he was about to end.

Without a word, she motioned for him to move, so she could get by with the hot tray of overly browned cookies.

"Kennedy?" He touched her upper arm as she slid the spatula under each cookie and placed it with more care than needed onto the cooling rack.

When she turned to face him, her breath escaped. Damn he was so good looking, too attractive for his own good.

"You don't owe me any kind of explanation. We hooked up, have chemistry here…" she motioned back and forth between them with her hand. "It's cool." She hoped her one shouldered shrug was casual.

"I think it's more than just chemistry."

He cupped her face and took her mouth with his. The kiss intensified until she could barely keep from yanking him to the bedroom. Somehow she found the strength to push away.

"I can't." Kennedy leaned her forehead into the center of his chest. "I can't do the casual thing. I want more, I hate to admit it. Totally get it that relationships are not your thing."

His hands slid down her arms and he pulled her against him. The solidity of his large body was so perfect, it almost made Kennedy settle in and ask him to stay longer. There was nothing she wanted more at the moment than to have him for her own.

But Frederick Edwards was about to walk out of her life forever.

Kennedy pushed away and turned. She grabbed a cookie and her teacup and went to the table. "So what did you decide as far as purchasing the ranch? I need to know so I can meet with a realtor in a couple months and put it on the market."

"Do you really want to move? To leave your land?"

Outside snow had begun to fall, fat flakes fluttered down creating a magical scene. In the distance cows ambled toward a shelter with the usual pace of not having a care in the world.

"I'm going to sell it."

He rounded the table to the opposite side seeming to understand she needed the distance. "I will buy it on a couple of conditions?" He lifted the papers and slid them to her. "I will pay the amount there, the deal must include the goats. Even Arnold."

Her eyes rounded and mouth fell open. He offered her ten percent more than asking price.

"Why would you want the goats? Arnold is spoiled, he won't understand being left outside."

"Understood." Rick kept his gaze on her. "What's your reply?"

She looked toward the screened in porch where Arnold slept on a dog bed. The little goat had a small ratty blanket he'd dragged there with him.

"I don't know that I can leave him. I'd already planned on a house with a yard for him."

"You haven't asked me what the second condition is?" Rick's eyes narrowed and Kennedy swallowed. The cows. Would he insist Sandra and Julia be sold or released to roam with the rest of the herd?

Her voice trembled. "What is it?"

He let out a long breath. "I'm not trying to make you upset. My intention is to make things easier for you. I know you love the goats, especially Arnold, and those two overweight pampered cows."

However… the word hung in the air. She straightened her shoulders. "Look, just know that I won't leave Arnold and I won't sell to someone who wants to slaughter the other goats or Sandra and Julia. I don't know what I'll do to keep them safe, but Lucy and I are coming up with a plan."

His lips twitched. "Is that so?"

With a firm nod, she pushed the papers back. "Yes. No deal. Now if that is all, why don't we just say our good-byes? I appreciate your help around the ranch…" Kennedy stopped talking when he stalked around the table and took her by the upper arms.

This time his eyes were light when scanning her face and his lips were turned up at the corners. "Don't get all mad at me. I'm trying to tell you the second part."

"What is it?" Her shoulders fell and Kennedy dragged her gaze from his tempting mouth. "What was your second condition?"

"That you stay here and live with me."

"What?"

"I'm screwed, can't seem to even look at another woman sideways without feeling guilty. I need you in my life Kennedy Brooks. Can't fathom a day without seeing you. If you'll accept a fucked up, scared shitless guy, I promise to do my best by you."

Her mind went into a thousand directions. Live together? Is that what he was proposing? Was he asking for a relationship? A commitment? Was he promising monogamy?

"Live together?"

"Yes."

"Relationship?"

"Mmm hmmm." His lips twitched and he lifted an eyebrow.

"Monogamy?"

"Definitely."

"Commitment?"

"I'll go get a ring."

"Say what?"

CHAPTER FIFTEEN

✦

Rick had to admit, getting Kennedy to listen to him proved to be hard work. She sunk into the chair and played with the cookie on the napkin until it broke into tiny pieces. Brow furrowed, she looked up at him while he gave her time to digest his proposition.

Eloquence was not his strong suit. Best to make a better attempt. "Look I don't expect us to move in together right away. I'd like to buy the ranch so you don't have to worry that I am only dating you to get it. Once that's done, you continue to live here. I can stay in the studio until we get more comfortable."

"We've known each other, what three weeks?" she asked and let out a breath. "I do feel strongly about you and would definitely like a relationship."

He knew her enough to wait for what else she'd say and not jump to any conclusions. Kennedy was definitely the opposite of him and he admired the trait. Impulsiveness had gotten him into trouble so many times.

This time, the decision to be with her was not impulsive. Hell, if anything, he'd fought it for days.

A light touch on his hand brought his attention to her upturned face. "Don't you think we're complicating things with the land deal? Let's take that off the table. I want to get to know you, to date, and see where our relationship goes. I have until spring to decide what to do about this place. I would rather we concentrate on us for now." Her lips turned up at the corners crinkling the sides of her eyes into a dazzling look. "Now would you please kiss me?"

Kennedy jumped to her feet and threw her arms around his neck, their mouths instantly pressed together. The hard thumps of his heart echoed up blocking his ability to hear anything, and Rick hoped Kennedy couldn't hear how scared he'd been she would turn him down. The tightness around his chest loosened and his shoulders fell as he wrapped his arms around the beauty who'd accepted him.

And boy didn't that just make him feel like the luckiest bastard around. After all he'd done, this was one gift he never expected.

Six months later…

THE HORSE NICKERED and stopped, its long neck bent down as it began grazing on the plush green grass.

As far as the eye could see, there was green. The hills to the east now covered in blue Astor seemed to reflect the color of the sky. To the opposite side, cows grazed and Rick caught sight of Julia and Sandra with the calf between them. The cows protected the little bugger as if it were the most prized of possessions. In a way, he supposed for them it was.

The sun shined and the gold ring on his left hand shimmered taking his attention. Who would have guessed that seven months after ruining his sister's wedding he'd be a groom himself?

Although his and Kennedy's wedding had not been as elaborate, he wouldn't have had it any other way.

They'd had a simple outdoor wedding, which much to everyone's amusement included Arnold as the wayward ring bearer.

Now as he looked across the open space toward where the ranch house was, Rick wondered what to do about the newest development.

A crazy feeling he'd never had before had grown to the point where he'd not been able to stand it. Finally, the night before, he'd told Kennedy what he wanted. To say she'd been shocked was an understatement. She'd asked him several times if he was sure.

Of course in typical Kennedy fashion, she'd not replied to his crazy request and instead promised to think about it and answer him today.

"Hey, you forgot your cell in the stables," Harvey called out as he neared on a four-wheeler. "It's been ringing."

Rick dismounted and walked to where Harvey stopped. "Thanks."

"The buyer should be here in an hour. I better head on back." Harvey circled and drove off. That afternoon, they were selling fifty head of cattle. Rick had decided to purchase horses and turn the ranch into a training camp. It would be easier to teach riding, roping, and such than to take a chance Kennedy would start naming more cows.

His phone dinged and he looked at a display. His mouth feel

open and laughter erupted. "Yes!"

Okay, let's try for a baby.

I love you.

THE END.

EXCERPT FROM JADED: LUKE

CHAPTER ONE

★

THERE WERE FEW things that scared Luke Hamilton shitless, even fewer the times anyone had intimidated him. At six foot, four and two hundred and twenty pounds of solid muscle, he couldn't remember the last time he'd felt nervous.

Of course, it didn't hurt that there was little he gave a shit about most days.

However, the situation at the moment was a bit unsettling. The coolness of a gun's muzzle at his temple didn't exactly give him a warm fuzzy.

"Give me your wallet," the gravely voice, combined with the stale breath of someone who'd not owned a toothbrush in possibly years, made his blood run icy.

Luke's control was tenuous at best on a regular basis, now with the situation at hand, the hold was quickly unraveling. If this idiot didn't move away soon, Luke wasn't sure he could stop from killing the bastard.

Too consumed with getting his next fix, the gunman let out a low growl. "What you waiting for? Have a death wish? Give me your damn wallet."

The surroundings slowly turned to tones of grey and black, all sound except his heartbeat vanished, and his hands curled into fists.

And now fear decided to make an appearance along with his buddy, the shakes.

"I'm warning you, get away from me." Luke's voice sounded detached and calm, almost as if he'd asked the time or the weather.

The first sign shit was about to get bad.

"SIR, PUT YOUR hands behind your back." The officer, although polite, ensured to keep his distance.

Somehow he had to get control. Every movement he made, even taking shallow breaths, sent spikes of alarm to his unsettled brain. Luke pushed away from the wall of the dimly lit gas station, shaking so hard he could barely remain standing. Good luck on doing whatever it was the police office instructed.

"I'm a war vet. Got PTSD. Give me a second."

The chill in the air combined with his sweat drenched t-shirt didn't help Luke regain control and his teeth chattered. Yeah, the whole junkie vibe didn't help his chances of getting the police officer to believe him.

"Put your hands behind your back now." The order this time was harsher, and Luke prayed the man would not keep pushing and send him back to shitsville.

Measured footsteps crunched on the gravel and he caught a glimpse of a second pair of black service shoes moving closer. Luke looked up as an older officer joined the first. The familiar eyes met his for an instant.

"What the hell did you do now?"

The first officer didn't lower his gun. "You know him? He about beat a guy to death. Poor sap is on his way to the ER."

Detective Johnson, who Luke had met at the local watering hole, came closer but stopped a couple feet away, giving Luke enough room not to feel crowded. The detective's concerned gaze moved from his bleeding knuckles to Luke's face. "You gotta do something. I thought you agreed to get counseling."

"I did. I went to the VA. They didn't do much more than throw pills at me." Luke turned to the other officer. "I'll get in the back of the car, but no handcuffs."

"Can't let you do that," the officer replied without hesitating. "Against policy. You're under arrest."

Luke knew the rules. Not the first time this had happened. Finally he let out a breath and lowered his shoulders. "Okay."

"I'll do it," Johnson said over his shoulder to the other officer.

Understanding how fragile Luke's hold on reality was, Johnson talked to him the entire time as he handcuffed his wrists behind his back. The words sunk in as Luke worked on regulating his breathing in hopes his body would follow suit.

"Thought you had family in Montana. Open country may be what you need. Nothing will get rid of the mess in your head Luke, but you have to do something before you end up killing somebody or…" He left off the rest. Johnson didn't have to say anything more.

There was always the permanent way out. There was only one guaranteed way not to have to deal with the fucking episodes that hammered at him constantly.

⭐

THE LONG DRIVE to Montana from the Dallas-Fort Worth area would take at least three days. There wasn't any hurry, not like anyone even knew he was headed there.

His family would welcome him home with no hesitation. Behind his back, they'd exchange questioning glances. His mother would fret wondering how long before he left again to not return for another ten years. Much like the old saying, "there's no place like home", it was true in this case.

His home was the only stable thing in his life. And also a stark reminder of how much he'd changed.

Luke appeared and disappeared when he felt like it. No need to explain where he was or what he did. His twin brother had made him promise to always keep the same phone number and answer when he called. The calls were infrequent, but often enough for his brother to know he was alive and not in some sort of state institution or something.

About every three months or so Tobias would call, their conversations lasting just a few minutes, enough for his twin to be assured and in turn ensure their parents were informed of his well-being and whereabouts.

So yeah, he had major issues. Hell, didn't most people have ghosts that came back to haunt them? So maybe the ghosts that disturbed normal folks were nothing like those Luke battled almost daily. Hell, his were more in the classification of demons. Fuckers rarely left him alone long enough to catch a break lately.

Even with music and the windows down, just after Fort Collins, he could barely keep his eyes open. For the past couple of hours, his stomach had been groaning and growling. He supposed the nuts and jerky, he'd eaten hours earlier, were not enough sustenance.

When the truck sputtered Luke glanced at the gas gauge and his brows flew up. "Damn it. Don't cut off on me now." He patted the dashboard and let out a breath when spotting an exit ahead.

He pulled off the interstate and thankfully there was a lone gas station on the right.

While filling up he glanced around noting there was very little around. The interior of the gas station had meager offerings. The last thing he wanted at the moment was more prepackaged crap.

So he paid for the gas, climbed back into his truck and cranked the engine. He turned away from the interstate onto a two-lane road. With the sun below the horizon, there was barely giving enough light to see the surroundings.

Just a couple miles later the perfect combination of a dingy motel and diner came into view. Once he reserved a room, he went straight towards the neon lights that spilled out over the blacktop. A greasy burger, some fries, and a beer would be a good way to end the day.

Other than an older couple, who no doubt drove the dilapidated RV parked across three parking spaces, the diner was empty.

When the bell over the door dinged, a thin pretty-enough woman, who stood at the counter, looked up. Her eyes widened just enough to let him know she was interested.

Sex would be good.

Luke settled into a tall chair at the long barely clean counter ignoring the older couple that craned their necks to look at him.

In their mind, he was either going to rob the place or shoot them. What was it about older people that they always suspected he'd do something stupid? Then again…

"Nice tattoo." The girl who'd moved to stand behind the counter looked at the upper arm tattoo that peeked from under the short sleeve of his t-shirt and then lifted her gaze to his. "Good work."

"Thanks." Luke ensured to look from her face to her chest giving the illusion he was actually admiring the view.

Judging by the lack of luster in her hair and skin, it was clear as day, she was as dead on the inside as he was.

With an empty gaze, from either working too many hours or a hard life, she tapped her pencil to the top of her pad. "Beer?"

"Got anything stronger?"

"Jack."

"That works. Also a burger and fries."

"Got it." She attempted a smile before turning and walking to peer though an opening to where he assumed was the kitchen. She lifted to her toes and called out the order.

With her ass poked out in his direction she looked over her shoulder at him. "On the rocks or straight up?"

TWO SHOTS OF Jack and a full belly later, Luke honestly didn't care if he got laid or not. Claiming her shift had ended, Jenny,

Tami or whatever her name was, sat next to him, perched on a stool, her left hand sliding up and down his inner thigh.

Okay that woke little Luke up, and he grunted while shifting in the chair.

"Want some company?" She leaned closer and pressed her lips against his. She tasted of Jack and mint gum. "Let's have some fun before you get back on the road."

She slid another shot in front of him and poured one for herself from the bottle she'd brought from behind the counter.

Luke nodded knowing she'd not ask any questions. Hell, she'd not even asked his name yet.

They slammed the shots down and headed to the motel next door.

As soon as they got into the room she lowered to her knees and began unzipping his pants. "Want me to blow you good?"

"Sure." He watched as she took him into her mouth and began sucking with enthusiasm, while her hands worked his length. Obviously experienced, she was good and didn't waste time, seeming to know exactly what it took to bring him close to finishing within a few minutes. His eyes practically rolled back by the time she slid his dick out of her mouth and stood.

"Damn you're hung." She tugged at her jeans, dragging them down without preamble and then pulled her t-shirt off over her head. Jenny or Terry, wasn't wearing a bra. Not at all abashed, she sat on the bed, legs dangling over the side. "Your turn. Take your clothes off."

He didn't waste time and undressed, ensuring to put his pants on a chair on the other side of the bed. After taking a condom out of his wallet, he leaned over and kissed her while stuffing his wallet under the mattress.

There wasn't much cash in the thing, but he needed his identification. One never knew with women like Amy or Terry.

Impatient, she took the condom from his hand and bit down, tearing the wrapping open. With swift movements, she sheathed him and peered up at him her eyes bright. "There, now get to work."

She spread her legs and Luke obliged.

It wasn't anything close to lovemaking, but more of a race to finish. Ensuring she was satisfied he fucked her until he finally lay spent on the bed with her sprawled over his chest. Interesting that the woman felt comfortable enough to fall asleep, her soft breaths fanning across his chest as he too allowed sleep to take him.

IT WAS STILL dark the next morning when he slipped out of the motel. Mary or Jenny was still fast asleep on her side, her tussled hair framing her face. The woman was pretty in a no nonsense kind of way. Whatever had brought her to this town was probably the same reason she'd not bothered to ask his name.

Luke didn't feel right leaving without at least some sort of goodbye, so he'd scribbled a quick note wishing her well and thanking her for a great time.

Whether a rancher, a highlander or a hunky cowboy, you will fall in love with Hildie McQueen's heroes!

Dear Reader,

I hope you enjoyed Brash: Frederick. I hope you continue on to read Jaded: Luke, another book in the Laurel Creek series. I guarantee you will love Luke!

He's Jaded…

Haunted by PTSD and a failed marriage, Luke Hamilton returns home to Laurel, Montana. Going home isn't an easy fix, but it beats ending up in prison or dead. At first the familiar surroundings and open land seem to set things right, but soon his old demons rear their ugly heads and he realizes it's the wrong time to enter any relationship.

Leah Morgan's experience in the corporate world has prepared her to prosper her father's ranch in Montana. She knows everyone expects her to fail, but nothing will stop her from turning the ranch around and selling it to the highest bidder – especially not a rancher. The quicker she closes the deal, the sooner she can get out of Laurel and move on with her career.

When Luke and Leah cross paths, they both discover that starting over can be a complicated business.

I have first hand experience to the changes that serving during wartime can cause. My husband and coworkers were all deployed to Afghanistan and Iraq when the war broke out. Two of my friends have died since returning. One of them took his life, the other one died of complications from an injury acquire there. The sacrifice of the brave soldiers, airmen, sailors, marines and civilians who serve sometimes continues after long they return.

I love hearing from my readers and am always excited when you join my newsletter to keep abreast of new releases and other things happening in my world. You can also follow me on Facebook and Instagram.

Newsletter sign up:
http://goo.gl/PH6D00

Facebook:
facebook.com/AuthorHildieMcQueen

Instagram:
instagram.com/hildiemcqueenwriter

Email:
Hildie@HildieMcQueen.com

Website:
www.HildieMcQueen.com

Printed in Great Britain
by Amazon